OXFORD
UNIVERSITY PRESS

Great Clarendon Street, Oxford OX2 6DP

Oxford University Press is a department of the University of Oxford.
It furthers the University's objective of excellence in research, scholarship,
and education by publishing worldwide in

Oxford   New York

Auckland   Cape Town   Dar es Salaam   Hong Kong   Karachi
Kuala Lumpur   Madrid   Melbourne   Mexico City   Nairobi
New Delhi   Shanghai   Taipei   Toronto

With offices in

Argentina   Austria   Brazil   Chile   Czech Republic   France   Greece
Guatemala   Hungary   Italy   Japan   Poland   Portugal   Singapore
South Korea   Switzerland   Thailand   Turkey   Ukraine   Vietnam

Oxford is a registered trade mark of Oxford University Press
in the UK and in certain other countries

First published in 1987
Reprinted 1988 (twice), 1990 (twice),1991, 1994, 1995, 1996, 1997
First published in paperback 1989
40 39 38 37 36
First published as a big book edition 1998
Reprinted 1998, 1999

British Library Cataloguing in Publication Data

Data available

ISBN-13: 978-0-19-272197-6 (paperback)
ISBN-10: 0-19-272197-6 (paperback)
ISBN-13: 978-0-19-271989-8 (paperback with audio CD)
ISBN-10: 0-19-271989-0 (paperback with audio CD)
ISBN-13: 978-0-19-272358-1 (big book edition)
ISBN-10: 0-19-272358-8 (big book edition)

Printed in China

Winnie the Witch

Korky Paul *and* Valerie Thomas

Oxford University Press

Winnie the Witch lived in a black
house in the forest.
The house was black on the outside
and black on the inside.
The carpets were black.
The chairs were black.
The bed was black and it had
black sheets and black blankets.
Even the bath was black.

Winnie lived in her black house
with her cat, Wilbur. He was black too.
And that is how the trouble began.

When Wilbur sat on a chair with
his eyes open Winnie could see him.
She could see his eyes, anyway.

But when Wilbur closed his eyes
and went to sleep,
Winnie couldn't see him at all.
So she sat on him.

When Wilbur sat on the carpet
with his eyes open, Winnie could see him.
She could see his eyes, anyway.

But when Wilbur closed his eyes
and went to sleep,
Winnie couldn't see him at all.
So she tripped over him.

One day, after a nasty fall, Winnie
decided something had to be done.
She picked up her magic wand,
waved it once and ABRACADABRA!
Wilbur was a black cat no longer.
He was bright green!

Now, when Wilbur slept on a chair, Winnie could see him.

When Wilbur slept on the floor, Winnie could see him.

And she could see him when he
slept on the bed.
But, Wilbur was not allowed to
sleep on the bed ...

... so Winnie put him outside
Outside in the grass.

Winnie came hurrying outside,
tripped over Wilbur,
turned three somersaults,
and fell into a rose bush.

When Wilbur sat outside in the grass,
Winnie couldn't see him,
even when his eyes were wide open.

This time, Winnie was furious.
She picked up her magic wand,
waved it five times and ...

... ABRACADABRA! Wilbur had a red head,
a yellow body, a pink tail, blue whiskers,
and four purple legs.
But his eyes were still green.

Now Winnie could see Wilbur when
he sat on a chair, when he lay on the
carpet, when he crawled into the grass.

And even when he climbed to the
top of the tallest tree.

Wilbur climbed to the top of the tallest tree to hide.
He looked ridiculous and he knew it.
Even the birds laughed at him.

Next morning Wilbur was
still up the tree.
Winnie was worried.
She loved Wilbur and hated
him to be miserable.

Wilbur was miserable.
He stayed at the top of the tree
all day and all night.

Then Winnie had an idea.
She waved her magic wand and
ABRACADABRA! Wilbur was a
black cat once more.
He came down from the tree, purring.

Then Winnie waved her wand again, and again, and again.

Now instead of a black house, she had a yellow house with a red roof and a red door. The chairs were white with red and white cushions. The carpet was green with pink roses.

The bed was blue, with pink and
white sheets and pink blankets.
The bath was a gleaming white.

And now, Winnie can see Wilbur
no matter where he sits.